Books by Paige Sleuth

Cozy Cat Caper Mystery Series:
Murder in Cherry Hills (Book 1)
Framed in Cherry Hills (Book 2)
Poisoned in Cherry Hills (Book 3)
Vanished in Cherry Hills (Book 4)
Shot in Cherry Hills (Book 5)
Strangled in Cherry Hills (Book 6)
Halloween in Cherry Hills (Book 7)
Stabbed in Cherry Hills (Book 8)
Thanksgiving in Cherry Hills (Book 9)
Frozen in Cherry Hills (Book 10)
Hit & Run in Cherry Hills (Book 11)
Christmas in Cherry Hills (Book 12)
Choked in Cherry Hills (Book 13)
Dropped Dead in Cherry Hills (Book 14)
Valentine's in Cherry Hills (Book 15)
Drowned in Cherry Hills (Book 16)
Orphaned in Cherry Hills (Book 17)
Fatal Fête in Cherry Hills (Book 18)
Arson in Cherry Hills (Book 19)
Overdosed in Cherry Hills (Book 20)
Trapped in Cherry Hills (Book 21)
Missing in Cherry Hills (Book 22)
Crash in Cherry Hills (Book 23)
Independence Day in Cherry Hills (Book 24)
Checked Out in Cherry Hills (Book 25)
Blackmail in Cherry Hills (Book 26)
Last Supper in Cherry Hills (Book 27)

Slain in Cherry Hills (Book 28)
Clean Kill in Cherry Hills (Book 29)
Targeted in Cherry Hills (Book 30)
Due or Die in Cherry Hills (Book 31)
Recalled in Cherry Hills (Book 32)
Arrested in Cherry Hills (Book 33)
Bad Blood in Cherry Hills (Book 34)
Burglary in Cherry Hills (Book 35)

Psychic Poker Pro Mystery Series:
Murder in the Cards (Book 1)

MURDER
in **CHERRY**
HILLS

PAIGE SLEUTH

CHAPTER ONE

Katherine Harper knew something was wrong when she opened her front door late Tuesday morning and saw Matilda sitting outside her apartment.

Kat scrunched up her nose as she looked down at the cat. "Matty, what are you doing here? You live next door."

Matilda stared back at her, her tail sweeping across the welcome mat.

Kat had to admit that Matty was a very striking cat. With her yellow-and-brown markings, white chin, and oversized green eyes, Kat thought the tortoiseshell was adorable.

But, contrary to what Matty liked to believe, she was a house cat.

Sighing, Kat brushed a brunette lock of hair away from her face before she scooped up the animal and started down the hallway to her neighbor's unit. "You know Mrs. Tinsdale doesn't like you out here. She fears somebody will steal you. And the landlord had a fit the last time he saw you in the common hallway. Now you're going to be in big trouble."

Kat shook her head, wondering why she was trying to reason with a feline. If anyone was watching, they'd assume she was desperate for companionship.

I need a boyfriend, Kat thought. Unfortunately, securing a boyfriend was a touch more difficult than stopping by the local grocery store and adding one to her shopping cart.

Kat made it to Mrs. Tinsdale's front door and adjusted Matilda in her arms to free one of her hands. But as she reached out to ring the doorbell, she noticed the door was already slightly ajar.

Kat froze, her pulse starting to pound. Mrs. Tinsdale never left her door open. Although Cherry Hills, Washington, didn't experience as much crime as Wenatchee, the nearest big city, leaving your front door open was still inviting trouble, even in a secured-entry building such as theirs. At the very least, nobody wanted to spend their hard-earned money running air conditioning for an entire twelve-unit apartment building in the middle of a July heat wave.

Kat looked at Matty, tempted to ask if she knew what was going on. Fortunately, she realized the ridiculousness of such a question before she voiced it aloud.

Her eyes locked back on to Mrs. Tinsdale's door as she set the cat on the floor. Something wasn't right about this situation, and every one of Kat's instincts was urging her to turn around and flee. But, given that Mrs. Tinsdale could be injured and waiting for help to arrive, Kat felt she had an obligation to investigate.

Kat poked her head around the doorframe. "Mrs. Tinsdale?"

Nobody responded. For that matter, Kat didn't hear anything at all except the hum of the air conditioner. She didn't know if the AC would drown out the sound of a burglar climbing through a back window and down the fire escape, but, if a burglar was in the apartment, she would prefer that he duck out now. Kat didn't care to run into anyone in the middle of committing a crime.

Stealing another peek at Matty—who

watched her with that disdainful look that cats had mastered over the years—Kat pushed the door open wider.

"Mrs. Tinsdale?" Kat called out again.

She stepped over the threshold when only silence returned. Looking around, nothing struck Kat as out of place in the living room. Neither did she see Mrs. Tinsdale anywhere.

Kat moved farther into the apartment, scanning the dining area and kitchen as she circled around the coffee table. Everything looked normal in those rooms too.

Taking a deep breath, she rotated toward the hallway.

A shadow flashed on the wall, causing Kat's stomach to leap into her throat. She whipped around, noting that Matty had followed her into the apartment unit. Her shoulders dropped three inches.

"You scared me," she scolded. Then, remembering how silly Mrs. Tinsdale always sounded when she talked to the cat, Kat spun around and refocused on her mission.

Kat moved down the short hallway and glanced into the first room. The unoccupied bedroom appeared to be ready and waiting for Mrs. Tinsdale's next guest. The duvet looked freshly laundered and put Kat's own rumpled sheets and unmade bed to shame. The only off-putting touch was the patch of fur smeared across the decorative pillows piled near the top of the mattress. Matty clearly thought the guest bed looked as inviting as Kat did.

The door on the other side of the hallway led to a small bathroom. Peering inside, Kat didn't see anything amiss there either.

She turned her attention to the closed door of what had to be the master bedroom. Assuming Mrs. Tinsdale was inside her apartment, that was the only place left where she could be.

Kat swallowed as she crept toward the end of the hallway. As much as she prayed that Mrs. Tinsdale had just popped out to do a little grocery shopping, she knew her neighbor would never have left Matty free to wander the building while she was away. Kat knew something was seriously wrong, no matter how badly she wanted to find a safe explanation for the open front door.

Kat paused when she made it to her destination. She gripped the doorknob, glancing back at Matty as if seeking the cat's permission to enter. Matty's eyes were huge as she stared back at her from the other end of the hall.

Kat positioned her ear closer to the door. "Mrs. Tinsdale?" she called again—fruitlessly, as she already knew there would be no response.

Left with no other options, Kat turned the doorknob. The hinges creaked as she slowly pushed the door open. She dreaded what she would find, but it wasn't until she saw the disarray in the bedroom that she realized she was holding her breath.

The rumpled bedspread dangled halfway off the mattress. She didn't know for sure if the mussed-up comforter had resulted from a scuffle or if Mrs. Tinsdale had simply not finished making the bed after waking up this morning, but she suspected the former. Mrs. Tinsdale struck her as the type to keep her living quarters neat and organized. Making the bed was likely one of the first things she did after waking up in the morning.

Kat's eyes veered toward the floor, where a lamp was smashed next to the nightstand. The disorder—and what it implied—made her woozy. She leaned against the doorframe for support, envying Matty and her position in the hallway. If Kat had her own way, she would plant herself outside as well, then wait for someone else to deal with this.

But she knew she couldn't turn around and walk away. Even if she and Mrs. Tinsdale hadn't known each other well, she couldn't leave a woman in potential peril simply to make things easier on herself.

Kat opened the door the rest of the way, searching the room for Mrs. Tinsdale herself. That was when she spotted the foot sticking out of the connected bathroom. The foot lay motionless on the floor, the ankle twisted at an unnatural angle.

Kat's heart was thumping so hard now she feared she might collapse without the support of the doorframe to keep her upright. She would need all her strength to make it from this side of the bedroom to the bathroom.

Her legs shaking, Kat clutched the side of the bureau, but she pulled her hands back as soon as they made contact. Too late, she figured it would be better not to touch anything. If it turned out that Mrs. Tinsdale's bedroom was a crime scene, Kat didn't want to leave any more evidence of her presence here than she already had.

Mustering up what remained of her internal strength, Kat somehow made it to the bathroom without leaning on anything. She had to smother a scream when she caught sight of Mrs. Tinsdale's face staring vacantly at the ceiling. Kat didn't need to check for a pulse or other vital signs. Anyone could see the woman was dead.

Dashing out of the bedroom with her stomach threatening to reject the breakfast she had savored only thirty minutes ago, Kat scooped up Matty on her way out of the apartment and rushed back to her own unit to call the police.

CHAPTER TWO

"Kat Harper?"

Kat spun around, her heart jumping when she spotted Andrew Milhone approaching from the other end of her apartment building's third-floor corridor. She hadn't seen him since they were teenagers, and whatever he'd been doing during their years apart, he looked good. He'd always stood six inches taller than her five-and-a-half-foot frame and still kept his sandy hair styled in a way that made it prone to falling over his forehead, but his shoulders were broader and his jaw more chiseled.

"Andrew?" she asked, unsure whether to believe her eyes. Although they'd both grown up in Cherry Hills, Kat had left as soon as she could and figured Andrew had done the same. When they were kids—both of them tired of the foster system they'd been thrust into—they had often talked about escaping from this place.

The hundred-watt smile she was all too familiar with was aimed straight at her as he closed the distance between them. She was pleased to note that he hadn't outgrown his dimples.

When he came close enough, he enveloped her in a hug. The gesture startled her at first—considering they hadn't seen each other in fifteen years—but she soon relaxed into him as his touch evoked pleasant old memories. Perhaps the best thing she could say about her childhood was getting to spend part of it with Andrew Milhone.

Andrew pulled back from their embrace and held Kat at arm's length. "What the heck are you doing in Cherry Hills?"

She shrugged, feeling self-conscious under his scrutiny. "I moved back a few weeks ago."

He tilted his head. "Moved back? I thought you vowed never to return to this place."

"I did," Kat said. She held her tongue as she looked around. She knew Andrew wanted her to elaborate, but she didn't feel comfortable explaining herself with so many strangers around. Between the crime-scene technicians processing Mrs. Tinsdale's apartment and the nosy neighbors crowding behind the yellow caution tape the police had strung up to keep the public away, too many people were liable to eavesdrop on their conversation.

Andrew seemed to sense her hesitation and didn't press for details. She was grateful for that. Even when they were kids, he had always had an uncanny knack for reading her perfectly. Of all the other foster kids she'd come in contact with while in the system, her fondest memories were those that included Andrew.

Andrew coughed, jarring Kat from her internal reminiscence. "This probably goes without saying, but I'm with the force now."

Kat eyed him up and down. "Why aren't you in uniform?"

"I'm a plainclothes detective."

Kat couldn't think of a response, too distracted by how appealing he looked in slacks and a button-down shirt. She'd never seen him dressed nice when they were kids, and didn't know whether to attribute the attraction she felt toward him now to his outfit or how well he'd matured in the past decade and a half.

"I entered the academy after community college," Andrew went on.

Kat forced her eyes back up to Andrew's. "How long have you been a cop?"

"Ten years now, a detective for almost two." He frowned, his eyes darting around. "But this will be my first homicide."

Kat couldn't say she was surprised. Cherry Hills didn't get much crime, let alone violent offenses. It made sense that Mrs. Tinsdale's case would be Andrew's first experience with a murder.

At least he wasn't working alone, Kat reasoned, taking in all the uniforms milling around. She wouldn't doubt that every officer in town was here. Cherry Hills didn't have a big force, so a felony of this magnitude would naturally command the entire department's attention.

Andrew cleared his throat. "So, you found her, huh?"

Kat nodded. "With Matty's help."

"Matty?"

Kat opened her mouth to reply, but her tongue froze when Andrew pulled a small notebook and pen out of his breast pocket. She hadn't realized this chat was official in nature.

Him suddenly adopting the role of interrogating officer when they had been enjoying an impromptu reunion just a minute ago threw her off guard.

Andrew poised his pen over the notebook. "Does Matty have a last name?"

Kat forced her thoughts back to the conversation at hand. Of course he was here in a professional capacity, she mentally chastised herself. What was she thinking, that he'd decided to pay a social call during the town's worst crime in who knew how many decades?

Kat gestured Andrew toward her apartment. "You can meet Matty yourself, if you'd like."

Andrew raised his eyebrows. "He's still here?"

"She," Kat said as she ducked into her unit. "Matty is a she. Her full name is Matilda." After making sure that Andrew had followed her inside, she aimed her finger at Matilda, who was lying on the couch. "That's Matty," Kat said. "I guess Tinsdale would be her last name. She's Mrs. Tinsdale's cat."

Matty eyed Andrew through slitted eyelids as if she were torn between giving him the stink eye and ignoring him completely.

"Do you think she saw what happened?" Kat

asked Andrew.

When Andrew didn't respond right away, Kat turned to face him. His lips were crooked, and his nose was scrunched up like an accordion.

Kat coughed. "I mean, Matty likely saw what happened, right? She could be an eyewitness."

"Kat, a cat can't be an eyewitness," Andrew replied.

"Why not?"

Andrew blinked. "Because there's no way for her to tell me what happened or to give testimony in court."

Kat planted her hands on her hips. "That doesn't mean she didn't see what happened."

Andrew's eyes flitted to the cat. "I take it you're going to adopt her."

"What?" Kat hadn't considered anything of the sort, only wanting to keep Matty confined to one area so she couldn't interfere with the police activity next door or escape outside.

"You plan on keeping her, right?" Andrew pressed.

Kat's hand floated to her chest. "Me? Why me?"

He shrugged. "You've always loved animals. Besides, she looks like she feels at home here."

Kat bit the edge of her lip as she studied Matty. With the cat curled up on one side of the couch, her tail tucked under her chin, Kat did have to admit she already looked as though she belonged here. Still, it had never crossed Kat's mind to adopt her permanently.

"If you don't want her, I can call Animal Control," Andrew offered.

Kat straightened, a cold current shooting down her spine with all the force of a lightning bolt. "Animal Control?"

Andrew sighed. "I don't like them any more than you do, but this cat no longer has a home. She has to go somewhere."

Kat's gaze drifted to Matty, who started languidly licking one paw, oblivious to the discussion concerning her fate. It hadn't occurred to Kat before now that Matilda was homeless, an orphan. The revelation sent a pang of empathy through her. If anyone knew about the pain of not having a family, Kat did.

And so did Andrew, Kat thought, looking at him as he jotted something else in his notebook. How many of the same foster families had they been placed with? At least three.

"I'll take her," Kat said.

Andrew nodded, not looking up. If her

announcement surprised him, he didn't show it. "So," he said, "what can you tell me about the events of this morning?"

Kat shifted her thoughts back to the matter of Mrs. Tinsdale's murder. "I was leaving to go grocery shopping when I saw Matty sitting on my doormat. When I went to return her, I noticed Mrs. Tinsdale's door was open."

"Go on."

"She didn't answer when I called her name so I went in search of her. That's when I found her in the master bathroom." Kat shivered and wrapped her arms around her middle. The memory of Mrs. Tinsdale staring at the ceiling with unseeing eyes inspired chills.

"You didn't hear anything suspicious before then?" Andrew asked.

"No, nothing."

Andrew moved to one side of the room and rapped on the wall with his knuckles. "The walls here aren't very thick. I can hear the team in the hallway."

"If she was attacked while I was in the shower, I wouldn't have been able to hear anything," Kat told him.

"What time were you in the shower?"

"Between nine-thirty and ten."

"And you didn't hear anything before or after that?"

Kat shook her head and sighed. Although she hadn't known Mrs. Tinsdale well, they had chatted on occasion. Mrs. Tinsdale had shared Kat's love of animals, as evidenced by her adoption of Matty and her volunteer activities for one of the local animal organizations. Who would hurt a woman as compassionate as that?

"What about the neighbors across the hall?" Andrew asked. "Do you think they might have heard something?"

"The other two units on this floor are both vacant."

Andrew's expression didn't change. If he was disappointed by the lack of leads so far, he didn't let on.

"Hey, Andrew," someone called out from the corridor. "Where are you? We're ready to move the vic."

Andrew walked over to the front door and poked his head outside. "I'll be out in a sec." He turned to address Kat again. "I need to go join the crew. I'll question you more later. In the meantime, here's my business card. If you think of anything crucial to the case, call my cell or just step outside and ask around until you find me."

Kat took the card he offered and slipped it into her jeans pocket. "I'll be here when you're ready."

"I'm counting on it." Andrew flashed her that smile again before disappearing into the hallway. Kat quietly shut the door behind him.

CHAPTER THREE

Five hours later, the commotion outside Kat's apartment began to die down. She figured the authorities had finally finished processing Mrs. Tinsdale's apartment. She had hoped Andrew would drop by again before he left, and found herself vaguely disappointed that he had departed without even a cursory goodbye.

Matty had spent the entire afternoon drifting in and out of consciousness. Kat was amazed that one animal could sleep so much. Although Matty had roused herself long enough to bathe at one point, she had promptly gone back to sleep as soon as she finished.

Now, Kat watched as Matty stood up and

stretched. "Did you see what happened to Mrs. Tinsdale?" she asked.

Matty turned her back to Kat and settled down again.

Kat groaned. There she went again, interrogating a cat and expecting an answer. She used to think Mrs. Tinsdale was strange for carrying on conversations with the animal, yet here she was doing the same thing. But she couldn't shake the notion that Matilda had witnessed what had happened earlier.

Kat thought about Andrew's claim that cats couldn't be eyewitnesses and wondered if it were possible to prove him wrong. Before she knew it, she found herself brainstorming on ideas to get Matty to share what she knew about her owner's fate.

Kat almost had to laugh at herself. When they were kids, she and Andrew were always competing about something. Now they were both thirty-two, and she was back to trying to prove him wrong not six hours after their first encounter in over a decade.

Still, if Matty *could* somehow communicate what she'd seen, maybe Kat could rest easier. She shuddered whenever she thought about a murderer skulking around next door with her sitting not fifty yards away.

Kat slumped against the sofa. "Poor Mrs. Tinsdale."

Matty twisted her head over her shoulder to shoot Kat a glare when the couch cushions shook. But before Kat could even consider apologizing, Matty rotated back around to rest her chin on her paws.

Kat eyed her new companion. That was one more thing she would have to get used to besides the murder: sharing her apartment with an animal. Kat had lived alone ever since she had been emancipated at age seventeen and learning to share her place—even if it was only with a cat—would require some adjustments.

Someone knocked on the front door. "Kat?"

Kat's heart rate sped up at the sound of Andrew's voice. She leapt off the sofa and rushed to answer the door, almost as if she feared he would stalk off if he didn't get a response within the second.

"I thought you left already," Kat said, surprised by how happy she felt that he hadn't ducked out without a goodbye after all.

"The crew already headed out, but I told them I had to stay behind to take your statement. Maybe you can give us some leads as to who might have done this."

"Oh." Kat wasn't sure what he expected her to say. Although they lived next door to each other, she and Mrs. Tinsdale had been more acquaintances than friends. But she *had* liked the older woman, and if she could help she would.

Andrew shifted, drawing Kat's attention to the items he had cradled in his arms. "Now that we've finished processing Mrs. Tinsdale's apartment, I gathered up all the cat things I could find."

"Thanks." She swung the door wide and motioned him inside. "Can I get you something to drink?"

"Water would be great," Andrew said, dumping the cat supplies in one corner of the living room as Matty pried one eye open to watch him.

Kat ducked into the kitchen, grabbed two bottles of water, and returned to the living room. After handing one of the bottles to Andrew, she settled next to Matty again.

Andrew sat down on the couch opposite them. "What can you tell me about Mrs. Tinsdale's day-to-day activities?" he asked, twisting the cap off his bottle and taking a huge swallow from it.

"Not much," Kat admitted. "I do know she spent quite a bit of time volunteering for Furry Friends Foster Families."

Andrew set his water on the coffee table and fished a notebook and pen from his breast pocket. "Furry Friends Foster Families?"

"It's a nonprofit organization that matches homeless animals with foster families until they're adopted permanently," Kat explained. "Placing the animals in a temporary home saves the organization from having to rent and staff a housing facility, and the foster families provide all the food and supplies. The organization really only needs to foot the bill for veterinary expenses."

"Makes sense."

"Mrs. Tinsdale was on the board or something," Kat said. "She called it 4F for short. I don't know much about it other than that."

Andrew glanced at her. "Really? That seems like the kind of thing that's right up your alley."

Kat shrugged. "I've been too busy looking for work and moving to take on anything else."

Andrew's head bobbed as he wrote something in his notebook. Kat itched to peek at his notes, wondering if he was jotting down observations about her.

"Did Mrs. Tinsdale get along with the other 4F volunteers?" Andrew asked.

"She seemed to," Kat said. "At least, she never said anything bad about anybody there."

"Do you know their names?"

Kat drummed her fingers against the armrest. "Imogene Little, for one. Mrs. Tinsdale mentioned that she was their president and most involved member."

When Kat remained silent for a long moment, Andrew said, "Anybody else you remember?"

"No, sorry." Kat felt sheepish over how little she could recall, but she and Mrs. Tinsdale had only chatted when passing each other in the hallway or sharing an elevator. Now, she wished she had spent more time talking with the older woman. "I only remember Imogene because she's lived here forever and I wait on her sometimes at Jessie's Diner."

Andrew's lips stretched into a smile. "You work at Jessie's?"

"Temporarily," Kat replied. "I needed something to tide me over until I find a job in my field."

"What's your field?"

"Computers."

"Yeah, you were always good with that stuff." Andrew leaned back and crossed his ankles, his face softening. "Remember when we used to save up all our change so we could sneak over to Jessie's and order the biggest milkshakes they offered?"

Kat laughed. "And Mr. and Mrs. Polanski were so nice they always gave them to us on the house."

Andrew grinned. "There are a lot of nice people in this town."

Kat stared at him, letting the old memories wash over her. He was right, there were a lot of nice people in Cherry Hills. She had forgotten that. She had spent so much of her childhood resenting the place where she was bounced from home to home like a ping-pong ball that she'd overlooked a lot of the town's positives. Returning to her hometown as an adult, she could better appreciate the old-fashioned hospitality that ran rampant throughout the area.

Andrew pushed his hair off his forehead. "Unfortunately, now we know there's at least one person in town who isn't so neighborly."

Kat's spirits deflated as she remembered the real reason why Andrew was here. "I just can't figure out who would have wanted to kill Mrs. Tinsdale," she mused aloud. "Why harm such a pleasant old woman?"

"That's the million-dollar question." Andrew tapped his pen against the notebook. "Did Mrs. Tinsdale talk to you about any recent arguments she'd had? Maybe she said something about a spat with one of the other 4F volunteers?"

Kat splayed her fingers. "She never mentioned anything like that. But we didn't talk all that often either."

Andrew pursed his lips, appearing deep in thought.

Kat crossed her legs, feeling inadequate over her inability to offer him more insight into her elderly neighbor's life. She leaned her head against the sofa and tried to remember what else she knew about Mrs. Tinsdale's activities. But other than 4F and her weekly trips to the grocery store, Mrs. Tinsdale didn't strike Kat as all that social. She glanced at Matty. That probably explained why she had adopted a cat.

Kat sat up straight, her heart lurching when she caught sight of the wall clock. "Oh, fiddlesticks! I'm late for work."

Andrew looked over at her. "Fiddlesticks?"

Kat smacked her palm against her forehead.

"It was something Mrs. Tinsdale used to say. I guess I picked it up from her."

One corner of Andrew's mouth twitched. "Mrs. Tinsdale was eighty-four years old."

Kat jumped off the sofa to mask her embarrassment over the exclamation. "I really do have to get ready, so, if you don't mind, you can see yourself out."

"Can I get your number first?" he asked. "You know, in case I have more questions."

"Sure." Kat rattled off her cell phone number.

"Thanks." Andrew flipped his notebook shut and tucked it and his pen back into his shirt pocket. "You have my card. Call me if you think of anything else that might help our case."

"I will."

Andrew stared at her for what felt like a fraction too long. "I'll see you around then." He grinned, those dimples of his cutting into his cheeks. "Welcome back to Cherry Hills."

"It's good to be back," she said.

And, for the first time since she'd set foot in town again, she realized it was.

CHAPTER FOUR

Jessie's Diner was a Cherry Hills fixture. Ever since Kat was a child, she remembered gazing wistfully through the glass windows from the outside of the building, wishing she belonged to one of the nuclear families dining inside.

Jessie Polanski had been fairly young herself when Kat was growing up. Jessie's parents had named their restaurant after their one and only daughter back when they'd first opened, a tribute that made Kat's heart ache with envy whenever she stopped to consider it. Now that Jessie was forty and managing the place, the diner had only become more popular. Jessie was an energetic woman who didn't mind working as hard as her employees. She still maintained her parents' legacy of treating each of her customers as if the business would collapse without their patronage.

"Sorry I'm late," Kat said now, bursting into the dining area where Jessie was wiping down tables. The intermingling aromas of marinara sauce and melted mozzarella assaulted her nose. She inhaled deeply. She could never get enough of how homey the diner smelled—especially when Jessie made her popular lasagna.

Jessie set her towel down and dried her hands on her apron. The brunette bun the slim woman always sported looked as though it needed some adjustment. The sight caused a flash of guilt to sear through Kat. She hated the thought of her boss having to work extra hard to make up for her tardiness.

"That's okay," Jessie said. "I heard about Hilda Tinsdale."

Kat tossed her purse under the bar counter. "I still can't believe it."

Jessie walked over to Kat, propped one hip against the counter, and grinned. "At least you got to reconnect with Andrew."

"Yes, that was one positive out of the whole mess." Kat hoped her pleasure over their reunion wasn't too apparent. She had forgotten how quickly word traveled in a town as small as Cherry Hills, and Jessie's Diner often served as the central hub for the area busybodies.

Jessie looked around the dining area. "Everything's under control out here. I'm going to help Lisa in the kitchen."

"Okay." Kat slipped an apron over her head and regarded her boss, wondering how much of the local gossip reached her ears. "Before you leave, you don't happen to know if Mrs. Tinsdale had any enemies, do you?"

"She didn't, as far as I could tell," Jessie said. "But I didn't know her all that well. She never ate here."

Kat nodded. She knew Mrs. Tinsdale had been on a fixed income and saved money by preparing all her meals at home. She'd mentioned once how she wished she could help her grown daughter out more but just couldn't swing it while living off her paltry social security stipend.

Jessie disappeared into the kitchen just as the bell hanging off the front door announced the arrival of a patron. Kat turned around to see Imogene Little breezing into the restaurant. The short, fifty-something woman was dressed casually in jeans and a T-shirt. Her auburn hair was pulled back in a ponytail and looked a bit mussed, as though she had put it up this morning and not bothered to redo it all day.

Kat watched as Imogene settled into a booth near the wall. Imogene was not only one of the biggest gossips in Cherry Hills, but she also served as the president of Furry Friends Foster Families. Kat remembered Mrs. Tinsdale commenting on Imogene's tireless passion when it came to fighting for animal rights.

The question was, if Mrs. Tinsdale and Imogene had found themselves involved in an altercation, could the same passion that made Imogene such a powerful advocate for animals have also driven her to kill another woman? Kat wasn't sure, but it couldn't hurt to question the other woman.

Gripping an order pad and a pen, Kat hurried over to Imogene's table. "Good evening, Ms. Little. How are you today?"

Imogene sagged against the back of the seat and rested one hand over her heart. "Why, Kat, I'm terribly heartbroken! I heard about Hilda. Such a marvelous woman! And how awful for you, finding her like that."

"It *was* awful, Ms. Little," Kat concurred.

"Please, call me Imogene," she insisted, bending forward to grab Kat's hand.

"Okay, Imogene." Kat wiggled her fingers out of the other woman's grasp. Displays of affection made her uncomfortable. "Mrs. Tinsdale often mentioned you when she talked about 4F. She really respected your dedication to animals."

"Oh, that sentiment was mutual." Imogene yanked a napkin out of the dispenser on the table and dabbed at the corners of her eyes. "I'm going to miss her terribly."

Kat took a deep breath, fortifying herself for her next question. "You don't happen to know if she had a disagreement with somebody recently, do you?"

"Oh, I can't imagine anybody fighting with her—or taking her life, for that matter! Whoever did such a thing must be a complete psycho."

Kat regarded the older woman. With her flushed face and the way she kept wringing the napkin in her hands, she looked genuinely distraught over Mrs. Tinsdale's fate.

"Such a senseless tragedy," Imogene went on, shaking her head. "Here in Cherry Hills you never expect something like this to happen."

"Mrs. Tinsdale didn't have any enemies at

4F?" Kat asked.

Imogene gasped, her right hand floating toward her chest as the napkin fluttered out of her grasp. "Heavens, no! Everybody in 4F gets along swimmingly. And we're in the business of saving lives, not ending them."

Kat had figured as much, but she still wanted to question the other 4F members. If some bad blood *had* existed between one of them and Mrs. Tinsdale, maybe Kat could pick up something during her inquiries. "Other than you and Mrs. Tinsdale, who else volunteered for 4F?" she asked.

"Willow Wu and Greta Opheim," Imogene said. "Fabulous women, both of them."

Kat jotted the information down on her order pad. Since this was the first time she'd heard their names before, she figured Willow and Greta must have moved to the area after she had fled town fifteen years ago. "What are their functions at 4F?" she asked.

"Willow is our secretary. She takes our meeting minutes and documents any issues reported by the foster families. Keeping a file on each animal helps us to match them with the right home."

"What about Greta?" Kat asked.

"Greta became our veterinary liaison this past spring. Given her local connections, she's a gem to have on the board."

Kat tilted her head. "Local connections?"

Imogene nodded. "Her husband is Dr. Harry Opheim. He owns and manages Cherry Hills Veterinary down on Culver Street. All the local vets give 4F a discount on their services, including Dr. Harry."

"He sounds like a great resource," Kat commented, making a note of the veterinarian's name and practice. Maybe he would have some information to share about Mrs. Tinsdale's personal relationships as well.

"Oh, he is. As the treasurer, Hilda dealt with him more than I did, but she always spoke highly of him." Imogene's shoulders sagged as though she were remembering Hilda Tinsdale's tragic fate anew. "Now I suppose we'll have to recruit somebody else to fill Hilda's spot, although it's really too soon for me to even think about replacing her."

Kat offered Imogene a sad smile. "I'm sorry for your loss."

"At least I didn't find her." Imogene shuddered. "That must have been a frightful sight."

Kat recalled the cold dread that had gripped

her body when she'd crept into Mrs. Tinsdale's
unlocked apartment, unsure what she would
find, and then the shock she'd felt upon spotting
her neighbor dead on the bathroom floor. The
memory sent an icy chill down her spine.

Imogene squinted up at Kat. "Don't tell me
you suspect Willow and Greta of having something to do with such an atrocious crime."

Kat slipped her order pad into her apron
pocket. "I'm merely hoping they can provide
some insights into Mrs. Tinsdale's case. I feel I
owe it to her to look into things a little, having
found her and taken in Matty."

Imogene's face lit up. "You took in Matilda?
That's fabulous! I was worried about that poor
little cat."

Kat smiled, thinking of Matty purring as she
had rubbed her goodbye. "Well, I couldn't have
her taken away by Animal Control."

"No, that would be horrendous," Imogene
agreed, "especially after the poor thing just lost
her mama." She tapped the tabletop with one
fingernail. "You know, if you need help paying
for Matty's first veterinary bill, we may be able
to assist at 4F."

"Really?"

"Technically the money is for the homeless

animals we foster, but since Hilda was such an integral part of our organization and you were kind enough to save Matty from an atrocious fate we could fund your initial visit."

"That's very generous of you."

"We have an agreement with all the vets in the area," Imogene said. "Go see any one of them, then bring me your bill. I live in the pink house on Spencer Street."

"I'll do that," Kat said, grinning.

"I believe Hilda frequented Dr. Mark's office down the block from you, but he could transfer Matty's records to any veterinarian you choose."

The front door bell chimed, drawing both women's attention away as an attractive middle-aged couple entered the restaurant, their arms linked.

Imogene elbowed Kat in the ribs. "That's Greta and Dr. Harry," she whispered.

Kat studied the couple. Greta Opheim was a very pretty woman, and, as evidenced by her designer jeans and chic blouse, she obviously knew how to dress to highlight her natural beauty. Her thick blond hair fell around her face and shoulders, giving her an almost angelic appearance.

Dr. Harry Opheim had a muscular build and

a full head of black hair. He stood close to six feet and carried himself in a way that suggested an easy confidence. If his veterinary practice wasn't successful, nobody would be able to tell from the image he projected.

Kat turned her attention back to Imogene, who had shifted her focus to her cell phone as it vibrated in her palm. "If you'll excuse me, I have to take this," she said. "You can get me a diet soda and the vegan nut burger."

"Sure, no problem." Kat inched away as Imogene answered her phone.

Kat ducked into the kitchen to relay Imogene's order before dropping off her soda and heading toward the Opheims' booth. Greta and Dr. Harry were hunched over the table, involved in what appeared to be a deep discussion.

"Welcome to Jessie's," Kat said, smiling at the duo as she walked up to them. "Can I get you something to drink?"

Greta leaned back in her seat to look up at Kat. Kat noticed the angry lines etched around the taut set of her mouth, and she had to wonder if the two had been arguing.

"I'll take an iced tea," Greta said.

"Water for me," Dr. Harry added.

The veterinarian didn't look nearly as upset

in Kat's opinion, but the dark bags under the eye she could see from this angle suggested that he hadn't gotten much sleep lately. Maybe he was too tired to work himself up into a lather.

"We know what we want to eat," he went on.

"Oh." Evidently the Opheims were all business, making it impossible for Kat to somehow work Mrs. Tinsdale into a conversation. She fished her order pad out of her apron pocket. "What can I get you?"

"I'll take whatever's on special," Greta replied, not bothering to look at one of the menus stacked behind the napkin dispenser.

"That would be lasagna," Kat informed her.

Greta reached up to rub the back of her neck. "Fine."

"Make that two," Dr. Harry chimed in.

"Will do, thanks."

As Kat retreated to the kitchen, she pondered over how best to broach the subject of Mrs. Tinsdale with the Opheims. Preferably, she could find a way to speak with Greta and Dr. Harry separately in order to eliminate the chance of one partner influencing the other's responses.

She considered what Imogene had said about 4F paying for Matty's initial vet visit.

Tomorrow morning struck her as the perfect time to get her new pet checked out by one of the area veterinarians.

CHAPTER FIVE

Cherry Hills Veterinary occupied one corner of a small shopping complex six miles from Kat's apartment building. She had intended to visit the establishment first thing Wednesday morning in the hopes that she could catch Harry Opheim while he was still fresh and more likely to entertain questions concerning Mrs. Tinsdale.

Unfortunately, Matty was having none of it. Kat had already wasted close to half an hour trying to coax the ornery creature into her carrier, a task that was proving more difficult than Kat had ever imagined it could be.

"Here, Matty," Kat crooned for the hundredth time, reaching under the bed, where

Matty had taken to hiding in one corner.

Matty didn't budge. She didn't even glance at the treat pinched between Kat's fingertips.

Kat sighed and rested her back against the wall. As defeated as she felt at the moment, she did have to admire the cat's determination. She would swear Matty had somehow figured out her vet plans, and she realized she had no other option but to wait out the feline. When Matty grew hungry enough or couldn't hold her bladder any longer, Kat would leap into action.

Deciding that acting uninterested would be her best strategy, Kat left the bedroom. She hoped her absence would lull Matty into a false sense of security and encourage her to relocate to what was rapidly becoming her corner of the couch. When that happened, Kat would be ready.

Kat retreated to the living room and flicked on the television, humming softly so as to sound nonthreatening. Just as Kat had hoped, Matty finally poked her nose into the room two television programs later.

When Matty jumped on the couch, Kat pounced.

Matty hissed as Kat's fingers encircled her body, but the squirming feline didn't claw or bite. Kat would have almost welcomed some injuries as she stuffed Matty into the carrier. As it was, her pet's refusal to lash out only exacerbated her guilt over tricking the animal.

"Sorry, baby." Kat secured the carrier door and poked her fingers through the holes to stroke Matty's fur. "I'm hoping this won't take long, but I need an opening with Dr. Harry. You're the only excuse I have to show up in his office."

Matty meowed crossly in response.

Twenty minutes later, Kat had located Cherry Hills Veterinary and was walking through the front entrance.

The redheaded receptionist looked up from her computer and smiled. "Hi there. How may I help you?"

"Hi." Kat lifted up the carrier. "I kind of inherited this cat, and I want to make sure she's healthy."

"Do you have an appointment?"

"No," Kat admitted, mentally berating herself for not calling ahead of time. She had been so anxious to talk to Dr. Harry she hadn't stopped to consider that he might be too busy to see her.

"That's okay," the receptionist said, tapping

on the computer keyboard. "You're lucky. We've been swamped all week, but we're pretty light today. No emergencies yet, knock on wood. I won't have any trouble fitting you in."

Kat breathed out a sigh of relief. "Great."

"May I have your name?"

"Katherine Harper. And my cat is Matilda."

The receptionist input something into her computer before gesturing toward a bank of chairs. "Okay, I've got you down, Katherine. If you'll have a seat, I'll let Dr. Harry know you're waiting. I'm Sherry if you need anything."

"Thanks, Sherry."

Kat turned around, but her steps faltered when she saw another woman already waiting in the lobby. It wasn't the unassuming blonde herself who made Kat hesitate but the huge Great Dane sitting beside her.

The woman smiled at Kat. "He's harmless," she said, stroking the dog's head.

Kat tried to return her smile. She didn't mention that she was more worried about Matty's reaction to the unfamiliar dog than she was about the Great Dane himself. Kat didn't figure Matty interacted much with other animals, given Mrs. Tinsdale's attempts to keep her inside.

But Matty simply remained hunched in one corner of her carrier as Kat sat down. Kat wasn't sure if Matty was too petrified to continue protesting her imprisonment or if she was becoming resigned to this whole situation, and she once again felt a pinch of guilt over her role in Matty's unpleasant morning.

"Kelly, Dr. Harry's ready for you in Room A," Sherry called out.

"Oh, goody." The woman with the Great Dane gave Kat a small wave as she stood up and disappeared down a short hallway, her dog trotting by her side.

Kat looked around as she waited. The lobby was clean, which pleased her. She had never been in a veterinary office before, and she had half expected the place to stink of urine or be overtaken by fur and dander. Yet, judging from the lobby, maintaining a sterile environment was as important here as it was in a normal doctor's office.

Sherry's voice broke into Kat's thoughts. "Katherine, Dr. Harry will meet you in Room B. Just go down the hallway to the second door on your left. Feel free to let Matilda out while you're waiting for Dr. Harry to show up."

Kat stood up and headed in the direction

indicated. "Okay, thank you."

The tiny exam room was also quite clean and smelled faintly of antiseptic. A small sink was built into the counter that stretched along one wall. A few glass jars containing cotton swabs, gauze pads, and the like sat on the counter next to a display of brochures that explained various pet diseases and treatment options. A metal table extended from the counter to the center of the room. Two chairs on one side of the table faced a rolling stool on the other. Kat presumed the stool was for the doctor.

She closed the door and set the carrier on the table. "You can come out now," she sing-songed, releasing the latch on the carrier door.

When Matty didn't emerge after several seconds had elapsed, Kat crouched down to get a better look at her. Matty remained pressed against the back side of her carrier. She glared at Kat before wrapping her tail tightly around her body.

Kat sighed. She couldn't blame Matty for being cross. After giving the cat a brief pat on the head, Kat sat down in one of the chairs, figuring it would be better to leave Matty alone. She would be pestered by the veterinarian himself soon enough.

She didn't have to wait long before Dr. Harry Opheim entered through a second door located on the opposite side of the room. Today he wore a white, calf-length lab coat over his clothes.

"Hi there," Dr. Harry said, grinning as he shut the door. "I remember you from Jessie's Diner. I'm Dr. Harry."

Kat did a double take when she got a good look at the doctor's face. The bags under his right eye that she'd written off to fatigue the day before had transitioned into a full-blown black eye overnight.

"I apologize for my appearance," he said. "I had a little trouble subduing one of my larger patients yesterday. Some of the biggest dogs also turn out to be the biggest babies when it comes to getting their shots."

Kat stood up. "Oh."

Dr. Harry pointed to his eye. "This occurred during a skirmish with a distressed mastiff."

Kat didn't say anything, shifting uneasily. She wasn't quite sure whether to believe his explanation. Although Dr. Harry didn't seem bothered at all by his appearance or concerned with masking his injury, Kat didn't dismiss the possibility that his nonchalance was forced. It wasn't a stretch to imagine this strong man overpowering Mrs. Tinsdale yesterday morning —and perhaps suffering a few facial bruises in the process.

"All right then." Dr. Harry turned his attention to the carrier. "Let's just take a look at little Matilda here."

Kat's mind churned as Dr. Harry stepped toward the table between them. Although she'd initially stopped by to determine what, if anything, Dr. Harry could tell her about Mrs. Tinsdale's relationships with his staff, this visit was quickly turning into a stealth mission to uncover whether Dr. Harry himself might have been responsible for the old woman's fate. That would mandate that Kat inquire about her dead neighbor a little more discreetly than she had originally planned.

Kat swallowed hard. The prospect of questioning a potential killer made her nervous, but, she reminded herself, she'd come here for answers, and she needed to work fast before the vet deemed Matty to be in good health and sent them both on their way.

Kat coughed. "So, Dr. Harry, I actu—"

Her words were interrupted when the door swung open again. Greta Opheim stepped into the room. "The computer's finally cooperating, so I printed out that information you asked for." She turned her attention to Kat. "Oh, hi. Jessie's Diner, right?"

"Yes." Although Kat was somewhat relieved by a second person's presence, probing the doctor for information had just become that much more difficult. "I'm Kat."

"Greta." She reached out to shake Kat's hand.

"Greta helps me out with administrative duties when she's not otherwise occupied," Dr. Harry said. He turned toward his wife. "I was just getting ready to examine Kat's cat." He chuckled, presumably over the alliteration. "Greta, since you're here, if you'll hold onto the carrier I'll get our newest little patient out in the open where we can meet her."

"Okay." Greta grabbed the sides of the carrier and braced her legs.

Dr. Harry slipped his hand inside the opening. "You ready for us, Matilda?"

As Greta steadied the carrier, Dr. Harry worked on persuading Matty to come out. The tension that Kat had observed between the couple yesterday didn't seem to be present now. Kat didn't know if they were simply acting professional for her benefit or if she had merely caught them in the middle of a fleeting disagreement yesterday.

A loud commotion diverted Kat's attention from her musings. Her stomach lurched when she saw that Matty was now thrashing inside the carrier, the structure rocking from her efforts despite Greta's hold on it. Matty couldn't seem to make up her mind as to whether hissing or howling would be the more effective way to communicate her displeasure.

Kat's protective instincts kicked in, and she took an automatic step forward. But Dr. Harry backed away from the table before she could interfere.

"My gosh," he said. "Your cat certainly doesn't want to cooperate today."

Kat felt another pang of guilt for using Matty as a prop in her investigation. "Maybe I should ease her out myself."

Dr. Harry nodded. "It might help if we left you alone for a moment." He set one hand on Greta's back and guided her to the door. "Perhaps she'll respond better with fewer people in the room. Why don't you work on her, and once you've succeeded prop the door open so I know you're ready."

"Okay," Kat agreed.

Matty calmed down after the Opheims left. Still, it took Kat a good ten minutes to convince the cat that it was safe to come out. After she shut the carrier and set it in one corner so Matty couldn't crawl back inside, she pried the doctor's door open a crack.

Dr. Harry returned two minutes later. He smiled at Matty, who had curled up in the sink. She flattened her ears back against her head in response.

"Are you going to let me have a look at you now, little Matilda?" Dr. Harry crooned, approaching the cat slowly.

"I'm really sorry about her behavior," Kat said. She looked at Dr. Harry's black eye again, willing to give more merit to his mastiff story now than she had been twenty minutes ago.

"Not a problem. Happens all the time." Dr. Harry reached for Matty, clamping his hands around her rib cage and lifting her gently from the sink. He set her down on a flat, plastic scale. "All animals react differently to stress."

Kat took a deep breath, sensing an opening. "Her stress might have something to do with the fact that her previous owner just died—and violently, I might add."

Dr. Harry glanced at her. "You're referring to Hilda Tinsdale."

"Yes."

Dr. Harry didn't say anything as he relocated the cat to the examination table. Matty let out a low, constant, growl, but she allowed the doctor to move her. Once she was on solid ground again, Dr. Harry slowly caressed the cat. He started with her head and proceeded past her neck and down her torso. Kat presumed he was checking for lumps or physical abnormalities.

Kat cleared her throat. "I think Matty—Matilda—witnessed the whole thing."

"Well, that would certainly help to explain her supremely agitated state," Dr. Harry replied, folding back one of Matty's ears and peering inside.

Kat shifted her weight to her other foot. "Did you work with Mrs. Tinsdale often?"

He pulled a stethoscope out of his coat pocket. "Not directly, no. Greta handles all the finances for us."

Kat absorbed that, unsure how she would go about verifying his claim. If he *had* killed Mrs. Tinsdale, he would understandably want to downplay the nature of their relationship.

Before Kat could think of something else to say to get Dr. Harry to open up, he released the stethoscope's metal bit that he had been holding to Matty's chest, unhooked the ear pieces, and slipped the device back in his coat pocket. "Well, Matilda looks to be in good health."

"Oh, thank goodness." Kat felt a weight lift off her shoulders. She hadn't realized until then how worried she was that he might find something wrong.

"Do you know if she's current on her vaccinations?" Dr. Harry asked.

"I'm not sure, but I can ask the vet that Mrs. Tinsdale used to provide a copy of Matty's records," Kat offered.

"Do that. I'd also advise you to consider a monthly parasite treatment for Matilda."

Kat's heart skipped a beat. "Parasite treatment? Matty has parasites?" She was surprised at how alarmed she felt. She'd only had Matty for twenty-four hours and already she was wholly in love with the cat.

"This would be an all-inclusive preventive treatment to reduce the risk of her contracting conditions such as heartworm, fleas, ear mites, and roundworm," Dr. Harry clarified. "Although there's no cause for concern right now, a single mosquito bite could change all that."

Kat tried to tamp down her panic as her gaze moved to Matty hunkered down on the examination table.

"There's no need to worry," Dr. Harry said, as if sensing her budding hysteria. "And the monthly treatment is easy enough to apply. You don't even have to bring Matilda into the office. Here." He rummaged in one of the drawers built into the counter and emerged holding up a cylindrical package. "You just squeeze this onto the skin at the back of her neck, where she can't lick it, and she's good to go for a month."

"That's it?" Kat asked, accepting the medicine with trembling fingers.

"That's it," Dr. Harry said cheerfully. "Normally I would apply it before you leave, but since Matilda is so agitated at the moment she might fare better if you treated her from the comfort of a familiar environment."

Kat bobbed her head. "Yes, definitely. I'll do that straightaway when we get home."

"Stop by the front desk on your way out and talk to Sherry," Dr. Harry said, reaching for the doorknob. "She'll let you know what you owe for today's visit."

"Okay. Thank you so much, Doctor."

Kat plucked the carrier off the floor, her mind whirling and her chest gripped by fear. Before today she'd barely known Matty. Now, the thought of losing her to parasites seemed like the worst thing in the world.

CHAPTER SIX

When Andrew stopped by Jessie's Diner later that afternoon for lunch, Kat asked the other waitress on duty to cover for her so she could talk to him. She couldn't wait to tell him about her morning visit to Cherry Hills Veterinary.

"I'm glad you're here," Kat said, sliding into the booth seat opposite him. She set down the strawberry milkshake she'd just finished making and pushed it across the table. "This is for you."

Andrew's face lit up. "What's the occasion?"

Kat shrugged, feeling self-conscious all of a sudden. "I guess I just assumed you'd want it, since we always ordered them as kids."

He grinned. "Oh, I definitely want it."

Kat found herself mesmerized by Andrew's long, masculine fingers as he gripped the milkshake glass. She forced her gaze back up to his face, hopefully before he noticed her staring. "So, um, I have some interesting news for you. Guess who in town has a huge black eye that appeared overnight."

"Who?"

"Harry Opheim."

"You mean Dr. Harry, the veterinarian?"

Kat nodded. "He said he sustained the injury during a wrestling match with a dog, but I'm not sure I buy it."

"What were you doing talking to Dr. Harry?"

"I took Matty in for a checkup this morning," Kat explained. "And, get this, she went all crazy when Dr. Harry touched her."

"She probably doesn't enjoy going to the vet," Andrew reasoned.

"She certainly didn't want to get into her carrier," Kat admitted, remembering Matty's scowl as she hid under the bed. "But still, the way she lashed out I'm pretty sure this was more than just an aversion to doctors. I'm wondering if Matty witnessed Dr. Harry attacking Mrs. Tinsdale yesterday morning."

Andrew shook his head. "That's impossible. Dr. Harry has an alibi for yesterday."

Kat's forehead furrowed. "He does?"

"Yes. His number was the last to appear in Mrs. Tinsdale's call history, so I checked out his story right away."

"What did he say?" Kat asked.

"That he never left the office until closing time," Andrew replied. "I also spoke with Sherry Peterson, his morning receptionist, and she confirms he was there from the time they opened at eight A.M. until she left at one P.M. Mrs. Tinsdale was killed sometime between nine and eleven."

"Maybe Dr. Harry snuck out for an early lunch," Kat proposed.

"He never broke for lunch," Andrew countered. "They were so swamped he just wolfed down a granola bar or two whenever he found a spare moment. And the clients who were there before noon all claimed that Dr. Harry was present for their appointments and that they never saw him leaving the building."

Kat frowned, not ready to give up the notion of Dr. Harry's guilt yet. "If he was only gone for a few minutes, they might not have noticed that he left."

"It would have taken him at least half an hour to get to your apartment building, involve himself in an altercation with Mrs. Tinsdale, and return to the office," Andrew said. "And as busy as his practice was on Tuesday, somebody would almost have to have seen him leaving the premises."

Kat absorbed that, her spirits deflating. Since she'd left the doctor's office several hours ago, she'd convinced herself of Dr. Harry's guilt. Now she was back to square one when it came to gathering leads on who could have killed Mrs. Tinsdale.

"What did he say about Matty, anyway?" Andrew asked. "Is she okay?"

"Oh, she's fine," Kat said, tamping down the fear that washed over her whenever she was reminded of Dr. Harry's parasite comments. "If you want to know the truth, I really only took her to the vet so I could hear what Dr. Harry had to say about Mrs. Tinsdale's relationships with his staff. I figured she had to deal with some of them because of her position on the 4F board." Unfortunately, after Kat had gotten it into her head that Dr. Harry himself could be guilty, she had abandoned any line of questioning concerning the other Cherry Hills

Veterinary employees.

Andrew's eyes narrowed. "Kat, you're not sticking your nose into this case, are you?"

She drew herself up. "What if I was?"

"Then I'd have to remind you that a homicide investigation is police business."

"I know that. And the last thing I want to do is interfere."

Andrew pulled his milkshake closer. "Good."

"But I have been . . . looking into things a little," Kat continued.

Andrew stared at Kat across the table, the sip of strawberry shake he had sucked up his straw falling back into the glass as his lips parted. "You've been looking into things?"

She nodded.

Andrew set his palms flat on the table. "Kat, you do realize that involving yourself in this case could be dangerous, right?"

She shifted in her seat. "I feel obligated to do something."

He regarded her for a long moment. "It's because you found her, isn't it?"

"In part, but also because Matilda lives with me now. I owe it to her."

Andrew blinked. "You owe it to a cat to investigate a murder?"

"Not just any murder, Mrs. Tinsdale's." Kat paused, trying to figure out how best to put into words exactly how she felt. "It's like Matilda lost her mother yesterday. Now that I've adopted her, I feel it's my responsibility to bring her justice."

Andrew's face softened. Kat knew what he was thinking. He figured she was equating Matty's loss of her mother with Kat's nonexistent relationship with her own mother. And, deep down, she knew he was right. She had always felt partially adrift in her own life, and she often wondered if growing up with a mother would have prevented that.

Andrew cleared his throat. "Kat, I should tell you that until we know who did this, we have to view everybody as a suspect."

Kat raised her eyebrows. "Everybody?"

His gaze didn't leave hers. "Yes."

She folded her arms across her chest, challenging him with her eyes. "So, you're treating me like a suspect?"

"Technically, yes," he replied evenly. "Since you're known to have been inside Mrs. Tinsdale's apartment around the time of her death, we have to consider the possibility that you're responsible."

A burning sensation spread throughout Kat's chest. "But I found her! And I called you guys as soon as I did. What was I supposed to do, just leave her there?"

Andrew shrugged. "I'm just telling you what our procedure is."

"Andrew," she said, dropping her elbows on the table and bending toward him. "We grew up together. You know I wouldn't have killed Mrs. Tinsdale. Besides, what would be my motive?"

"Kat, I'm obligated to follow procedure, whether or not I know you."

She gawked at him. Although she knew he was only doing his job, she couldn't help but feel stung by his words. Worse, from the way he talked, he sounded as though he had no problems treating her as he would a potential murderer.

Andrew slid his milkshake aside and hunched over the table. "Kat, I hope you understand that our consideration of you as a suspect is just standard procedure. You're not even a suspect really, just a person of interest."

Kat didn't see the difference, but she didn't care to belabor the point either. "I understand," she said instead. "But that makes it all the more important that I help find the real killer, don't you agree?"

Andrew sighed. "Well, I can't tell you what to do on your own time."

Kat let out a breath. "Great, than—"

"But I also can't condone you interfering with an active police investigation," Andrew continued, his face stern.

Kat's eyes widened. "Oh, I'm not trying to interfere. I'm trying to help."

"That's what I'm afraid of," Andrew mumbled just before Kat slipped out of the booth to return to work.

CHAPTER SEVEN

Noise from the other side of her bedroom wall awoke Kat late that night. She sat up and listened quietly, unsure whether she had actually heard something or merely dreamed it. But the faint sounds indicative of someone moving around next door didn't fade as the seconds ticked by. Not only that, but her bedroom shared a wall with the master bedroom of Mrs. Tinsdale's apartment. Whoever was next door was currently bumbling around where a woman had recently been murdered.

Blood rushed through Kat's ears as her adrenal glands revved up. Deciding she wouldn't get any sleep until she saw for herself exactly what was going on next door, Kat eased out of bed, pulled on her bathrobe, and crept into the living room. Flicking on a light, she glanced around for a makeshift weapon. She wasn't about to wander into what had been an active crime scene not forty-eight hours ago without something she could use to defend herself.

And staying in her own apartment wasn't an option. She was too curious to find out who was in Mrs. Tinsdale's unit and what they were doing there. Plus, she had to admit, that old childhood stubborn streak that flared whenever she disagreed with Andrew blazed stronger than ever after he'd tried to get her to stop looking into things. She hated for anyone to tell her what to do, even if she knew they were only concerned about her safety.

Kat paced around the living room as she searched for potential weapons. Her steps halted when she saw Matty watching her from the sofa.

"What?" she said, her defenses rising. "You want me to sit here and not do anything?"

Matty turned her head as though to dismiss Kat and her nosy ways.

There I go again, Kat thought, *trying to reason with a cat.*

Refocusing on her mission, Kat ignored

Matty and looked around the room once more. She finally settled on the universal remote that could control every electronic device in her apartment if only she could figure out how to program the thing correctly. The remote wouldn't do her much good against an armed intruder, but it was better than nothing, and carrying a butcher knife around seemed too extreme.

Kat briefly considered calling Andrew before she left, but it was three o'clock in the morning and she would hate to disturb him this late unless she really needed help. Besides, she knew he would tell her to stay put until he arrived, and whoever was next door might be halfway to Wenatchee before Andrew even finished getting dressed.

Her heart pounding, Kat pried the front door open and stuck her head into the corridor. She could tell Mrs. Tinsdale's door wasn't shut completely from the way the light inside spilled into the dimmer common hallway. The open door led her to believe that the person currently trespassing wasn't worried about anyone catching them. That eased some of her fears.

Clutching the remote, Kat crept toward Mrs. Tinsdale's unit. She paused just outside the door when she spied a middle-aged brunette woman sitting on the couch as she shuffled through a stack of papers on the coffee table. Dressed simply in jeans and a T-shirt and with no obvious weapons in sight, the woman looked harmless enough.

Kat hesitated only briefly before knocking on the door, keeping her knees bent as she did so. In case she was wrong about her assessment of the intruder, she wanted to be prepared to sprint back to her own apartment.

The woman's head snapped up, her eyes wide as they locked on to Kat's. "Who are you?"

Kat braced her feet and pushed the door open wider. "I could ask you the same thing."

The woman stood up and planted her hands on her hips. "How did you get in here? This is supposed to be a secure building."

"I live here," Kat replied. "How did *you* get in here?"

"I have a key."

Kat raised her eyebrows. "You do?"

The woman eyed Kat up and down, a slight frown pulling at the corners of her mouth. Kat didn't know whether her questions or her disheveled appearance had prompted the woman's disapproving look.

The woman wrenched her eyes back up to meet Kat's. "I'm Betty Hamilton," she said.

Some of the fight left Kat's system. "You're Mrs. Tinsdale's daughter."

She had a flashback of Mrs. Tinsdale mentioning Betty during one of their hallway conversations. Mrs. Tinsdale had been upset after learning that her son-in-law had recently announced his plans to leave Betty for another woman after twenty years of marriage. Kat had forgotten the daughter's name until now.

Kat stepped into the apartment and held out her hand, but quickly dropped it back to her side when she realized she was still holding the remote control. She stuffed the remote in her bathrobe pocket. "I'm Kat Harper. I live next door."

"Oh, nice to meet you," Betty said, although her flat tone suggested she would have preferred if Kat had stayed home and minded her own business.

Kat looked at the papers on the coffee table. "What are you looking for?"

"Mom's life insurance paperwork."

Kat rocked backward. It seemed rather callous for Mrs. Tinsdale's daughter to already be searching for a financial windfall when her mother had turned up murdered not two days ago.

Betty seemed to understand how her words had come across. She bit her lip as a flush crept up her neck. "I know that sounds harsh, but I really do need the money, and me getting it sooner rather than later isn't going to bring Mom back."

Kat eyed the papers spread across the table. "Are those all her personal documents?"

"There's more in the bedroom closet," Betty said. "I only grabbed these to start. I brought them out here because I couldn't stand the idea of being so close to where she . . . where she . . ."

Tears sprang to Betty's eyes as she choked on her words. Under normal circumstances, such a raw display of emotion would have softened Kat's heart. However, after learning of Betty's motive for rummaging through her dead mother's files in the middle of the night, she had her suspicions that Betty Hamilton might only be acting grief-stricken so Kat wouldn't suspect her of something more sinister than just greed.

"It still doesn't feel real to me," Betty said, her voice hollow. "Mom's passing, that is." She looked at Kat for a long moment before turning away and grabbing a handful of papers off the coffee table.

Kat watched her, torn between volunteering to help and retreating back to her own apartment. She had to wonder if the promise of collecting Mrs. Tinsdale's life insurance money might have driven Betty to kill her own mother.

Betty derailed Kat's train of thought when she let go of the pages she'd picked up and covered her face with her hands.

"Ugh, this is all too much!" she wailed. She jerked her arms toward the documents. "Look at this mess! How am I supposed to find anything important here?"

Kat moved closer and lifted up one of the papers. It was an invoice from Cherry Hills Veterinary. She scanned over the itemized charges, noting the discount at the bottom labeled 'Furry Friends Foster Families.' "These are for 4F."

Betty peered up at her. "4F?"

"Furry Friends Foster Families," Kat said. "Mrs. Tinsdale volunteered on the board there."

"Oh, right. Mom talked about that little group, but I never really paid much attention."

Kat couldn't help but think that if Betty *had* paid more attention to her mother's stories she might not be in her current situation of trying to figure out Mrs. Tinsdale's filing system from scratch.

But Kat wasn't here to berate a grieving daughter. "If you'd like, I can sort through these with you to separate out everything related to 4F. I kind of know the president, so I can turn all this stuff over to her."

Betty's face brightened. "You would do that?"

"Sure." Kat still had her concerns about spending time alone with a potential murderer, but she rationalized that Betty had no motive to hurt *her*, even if she had killed her own mother. Besides, Betty *did* seem genuinely distraught, although Kat couldn't discern whether that was because she was having so much trouble locating the insurance paperwork or because of her recent loss.

Their attention was diverted when Matty came streaking down Mrs. Tinsdale's hallway, her paws scissoring in front of her as she raced toward the kitchen.

"Matty!" Kat yelped, her stomach leaping into her throat. She must have forgotten to close her apartment door when she'd left, and the cat must have followed her over here.

Once she recovered from the shock of the

interruption, Kat took a closer look at the animal. Matty was playing with something shiny,
batting it across the floor as though it were a
mouse.

Kat walked over to her pet. Matty looked
expectantly up at her, her tail swishing as if she
expected Kat to join in on the game. Stooping
forward, Kat spied the silver hoop earring half
trapped underneath one of Matty's paws.

Kat reached down and gently worked the
earring from Matty's grasp. Matty lifted her
haunches, ready to launch her body in whatever
direction Kat threw her new toy. Kat hated to
disappoint her, but right now she didn't have
time to play.

Kat examined the earring, her heart beating
faster as she absorbed the implications of its
presence here. The metal back that hooked onto
the sharp end of the pin was missing, leading
her to believe that the earring hadn't been delib-
erately removed from someone's ear. It also
didn't look like the type of jewelry that Mrs.
Tinsdale would wear. The older woman had always preferred simple, understated accessories.

Could Mrs. Tinsdale's murderer have un-
knowingly left this on Tuesday? Kat wondered.
When the police had searched the apartment,

they could have easily overlooked something this small.

Kat tucked the earring in her bathrobe pocket and made a mental note to call Andrew as soon as the hour turned decent. Until then, she might as well help Betty Hamilton sort through Mrs. Tinsdale's paperwork. She was pretty sure she wouldn't be able to go back to sleep no matter how hard she tried.

But first, she had a cat to return home.

CHAPTER EIGHT

Kat Harper had a lot to learn about cats. For one thing, she was discovering that Matilda pretty much did as she pleased, regardless of whether Kat approved. If Matty preferred to use the couch to sharpen her claws instead of the scratching post that Andrew had lugged over from Mrs. Tinsdale's apartment, she did. If Matty wanted to sit in the middle of the kitchen table, she plopped her butt down there even if it meant that her tail landed on top of Kat's microwave dinner.

Kat was also learning that she couldn't carelessly set things down as she had become accustomed to doing during her fifteen years of living alone.

After sorting through Mrs. Tinsdale's files with Betty Hamilton, Kat had returned home with a stack of paperwork for 4F. She'd set it, the remote control, and the earring in one neat pile on the coffee table, then proceeded to the bedroom, where she'd tossed and turned despite her best efforts to catch a few more minutes of shut-eye. When she finally gave up on sleep and emerged from her bedroom, she found Matty playing with her shiny new toy in the middle of the living room.

"Matty!" Kat rushed over and snatched the earring out of Matty's paws. "That could be evidence!"

Miffed, Matty sat on the floor and stared at her, her tail thwacking the coffee table legs with displeasure.

Kat shoved the earring into her bathrobe pocket and shook her finger at the cat. "You have plenty of other toys. Why don't you play with one of those?"

Matty turned her tail up and sauntered into the kitchen.

Kat sighed as she followed after her, knowing Matty was expecting her breakfast. That was another thing she was learning about cats. They were very regimented about their meals and didn't appreciate any delays when it came to being served.

Kat dished out some kibble while Matty twined between her legs. The affectionate display caused the last of Kat's exasperation to fade away. She would have given anything to have such a loving pet when she was a child. But that wasn't a possibility when you grew up in foster care. And, as an adult, Kat never found herself with a decent amount of free time to devote to an animal.

Of course, if Kat were honest with herself, she *had* had the time. What she didn't have was the confidence that she would be the best owner, and she feared she would end up doing an animal more harm than good. She had seen firsthand how a bad parent could cause more damage than no parent at all.

"Snap out of it," Kat mumbled to herself, shaking her head. "You have more important things than the past to focus on right now."

Like finding out who murdered Mrs. Tinsdale, Kat thought, touching the outline of the earring through her bathrobe pocket.

Checking the time, Kat returned to her bedroom for her cell phone and dialed Andrew. "I found something in Mrs. Tinsdale's apartment that you might be interested in," she told him when he answered.

"What were you doing in Mrs. Tinsdale's apartment?" he asked.

"I'll tell you when you get here."

There was a pause before Andrew replied. "I'll be over in half an hour."

Kat used the time before Andrew's arrival to take a quick shower and get dressed. She found herself fussing over her makeup more than normal, which both surprised and annoyed her.

"It's only Andrew," Kat told her reflection in the mirror. Then she grabbed a mascara wand and applied a second coating to her lashes.

When the doorbell rang, Kat catapulted off the couch as if she had been touched by an electrical wire. She made herself stand there for a moment, trying to calm the flutters in her stomach.

From her spot on the sofa, Matty stopped grooming herself to eye Kat, her head tilted to one side. Kat presumed her pet was just as perplexed by her behavior as she herself was. She'd never felt this way about the prospect of seeing Andrew when they were kids. Sure, she had enjoyed his company and always looked forward to spending time with him, but butterflies in her stomach? It was absurd.

I'm just anxious to show him the earring, Kat told herself as she swung the door open.

Andrew smiled at her, causing Kat's heart rate to spike. "So, what did you find?" he asked.

"A hoop earring," Kat told him. "It might have belonged to the killer."

Andrew stepped inside the apartment. "What makes you think that?"

Kat shut the door. "Because Mrs. Tinsdale didn't wear earrings like this one. I'll get it, and you can take a look for yourself."

She dashed into her bedroom and retrieved the earring from her nightstand drawer, where she'd hidden it from Matty before jumping in the shower. When she returned to the living room, she held it out to Andrew. She felt sparks as their fingers brushed during the handoff.

Kat sat down next to Matty, petting the cat to steady herself as Andrew studied her discovery.

After a moment, Andrew looked up at her. "You say you found this in Mrs. Tinsdale's apartment?"

"Well, actually, Matty found it," Kat admitted.

Andrew's gaze drifted toward the purring

feline. "What were you and Matty doing in Mrs. Tinsdale's apartment?"

"Betty, Mrs. Tinsdale's daughter, was here this morning," Kat explained. "I heard her rummaging around next door and went to check it out. Matty followed me, and later I saw her playing with the earring."

"Betty Hamilton came here this morning?" Andrew asked, arching one eyebrow.

Kat nodded. "She showed up around three A.M. looking for Mrs. Tinsdale's life insurance paperwork."

Andrew collapsed onto the unoccupied sofa. "That sounds like a pretty big motive for murder."

"Yes, but I'm not convinced she did it. You didn't see how distressed she was. At first I thought maybe she was putting on an act, but after spending all that time sifting through Mrs. Tinsdale's files with her, I believe she's truly grieving."

"Just because she's grieving doesn't mean she didn't kill her mother," Andrew countered.

"If she had killed her, wouldn't she be a little more discreet about wanting the insurance money?" Kat asked. "Everybody knows you don't start looking for a payoff the day after you murder somebody."

Andrew stared at her. "Everybody knows that?"

Kat flushed. "You know what I mean."

A grin tugged at Andrew's lips. "When did you get to be an expert on how murderers act?"

"It's common sense," she retorted. She felt her own smile materializing. She had to admit, it felt good to be teased by her childhood friend again.

Andrew's mouth flattened out into a more serious expression. "However she feels about her mother's death, Betty showing up in the middle of the night to search Mrs. Tinsdale's apartment is a red flag. I'm going to have to question her again, and more seriously this time."

"I wouldn't expect anything less," Kat said. "But I don't think you're going to get anywhere. You'll just find out that she's hard-pressed for money after her husband walked out and left her with nothing."

"That may be, but she still might help to shed light on who *would* want her mother dead." He paused. "Do you know if Betty and Mrs. Tinsdale had a good relationship?"

Kat lifted one shoulder. "As much as most

mothers and daughters, I suppose."

She ignored the pang in her heart as she delivered the statement. She would have given anything to have any type of relationship, average or not, with her own mother. As it was, she knew very little about the woman.

Andrew coughed and sat up. "Well, people have been known to kill their loved ones for a lot less than a life insurance payout."

"How much is Betty owed?"

"I don't know. I'll have to get one of the guys down at the station to look into it."

Kat sat bolt upright when she noticed the time displayed on the wall clock. "Oh, fiddlesticks!"

Andrew looked at her, his dimples threatening to make another appearance. "Again with the fiddlesticks?"

Kat leapt off the sofa. "I just realized I have to be at work in forty minutes, and I still need to stop somewhere first."

Andrew spread his hands. "Don't let me keep you from anything."

Kat backed into the hallway. "Sorry to run off on you like this."

Andrew stood up and headed toward the front door. "No problem. I'll see myself out."

As Andrew left, Kat raced to her bedroom to grab a hair tie, but the one she typically wore to work was nowhere to be found.

She stormed back out to the living room, jamming her hands on her hips. "Matty, you weren't playing with my hair tie again, were you?"

Matty looked at her and yawned.

Kat groaned. There she went, questioning a cat again.

Oh, fiddlesticks, Kat thought. She was turning into Mrs. Tinsdale.

CHAPTER NINE

"Kat, hello!" Imogene Little swung her front door wide open and waved Kat inside. "I'm tickled to see you again."

Kat stepped over the threshold. "Hi, Ms. Little."

"Please, call me Imogene."

"Okay, Imogene." Kat held up the piece of paper in her hand. "I brought the invoice from Matty's vet visit. You said you might be able to help me cover the costs, remember?"

"Of course I remember!" Imogene closed the door and took the invoice from Kat's hand.

Kat had a flashback of sitting next to Betty Hamilton as they both sorted through Mrs. Tinsdale's documents. She had meant to bring

Imogene the 4F paperwork they'd found but had forgotten in her haste. She would just have to remember the next time she had a reason to meet with Imogene.

Imogene perused the Cherry Hills Veterinary invoice before smiling at Kat. "Nothing unusual here. I take it Matty is in good health then?"

Kat nodded, although she felt a tightening in her chest when she remembered what Dr. Harry had said about a single mosquito bite transmitting parasites. "Dr. Harry wants to give her some kind of medicine every month though, to ward off heartworms and some other things."

"Oh, that's typical," Imogene said.

Kat felt a bit better that the news didn't seem to alarm Imogene. Maybe monthly parasite treatments really were as commonplace as Dr. Harry had led her to believe.

Imogene bustled farther into the house, motioning for Kat to join her. "Did you pay these charges already?"

Kat followed her hostess. "Yes. I told Sherry, the receptionist, that you said it was okay to apply the Furry Friends Foster Families discount."

"Good." Imogene moved into a smaller room that appeared to serve as her home office.

"I'll just write you a check to cover your costs then."

"I really appreciate this," Kat said.

Imogene sat down and pulled a checkbook out of one of the desk drawers. "Don't mention it. You're a dear for taking in Matty." She fingered the edge of the checkbook cover, a melancholy look developing on her face. "It's times like this when I really miss Hilda the most. Normally she would be the one writing you a check."

Kat smiled sadly. "I'm sorry I didn't know her better. She seems like she really did a lot for the animals."

"Oh, she did, she did."

The sound of the doorbell caught the women's attention.

Imogene stood up. "If you'll excuse me, I'll finish writing you this check as soon as I see who's here."

"Okay."

As Imogene went to answer the door, Kat folded her hands in front of her and looked around the room. She had to admire Imogene's tastes. The furniture looked to be made of oak or some other expensive, sturdy wood. The desk crammed into one corner of Kat's own place had been constructed out of what she assumed was particleboard. She had brought it home in a box and assembled it herself.

". . . before the benefit dinner," Kat heard a woman say.

Imogene reentered the room with Greta Opheim in tow, a purse the size of a parade float hooked over one of Greta's shoulders.

"Kat," Greta said. "I seem to be running into you everywhere."

"She came by to get reimbursed for Matty's vet expenses," Imogene told her, returning to her chair and picking up a pen.

"Oh." Greta regarded Kat. "I didn't realize your visit yesterday was for 4F business. I was under the impression you had adopted Matty permanently."

"I did," Kat confirmed.

"I felt, given the circumstances, that we should pay for Matty's initial checkup," Imogene interjected, filling out the check and scribbling her signature on the bottom. "We do that for all the animals before we adopt them out anyway, and Kat here was a lifesaver to take in Matty the way she did after that awful tragedy."

"Oh, I wasn't complaining," Greta said. "But if I had known I could have saved her the hassle of paying first then getting reimbursed, not to mention her having to make the trip out here." She turned toward Kat. "Typically when Cherry Hills Veterinary does work for 4F, the foster families don't even see the invoices. I prefer not to burden them with that if I don't have to."

"Well, it wasn't any trouble," Kat assured her. "I was just happy you all were kind enough to cover this visit."

"We had to do something for poor Matty, after what happened to her mama." Imogene looked up at Kat, her face brightening. "Say, you wouldn't be interested in attending our benefit dinner next month, would you?"

"How much are tickets?" Although Kat didn't have much discretionary income at the moment, she wanted to repay 4F for their generosity. If seats were cheap enough, she would make it a point to scrimp a little in the next few days in order to attend. Plus, the money would be going to a good cause.

Imogene waved her hand. "You could take Hilda's seat, no charge."

"Oh, no, I couldn't do that," Kat protested. "Really, I don't mind buying my own ticket, as long as they aren't too far out of my budget."

"The tickets don't have a set cost," Greta

piped up. "They're based on donations, whatever you want to pay. But the minimum is
twenty dollars."

Kat relaxed. "In that case, I'd love to attend.
Just give me a week or so to come up with some
money."

"Absolutely." Imogene tore out the check
before standing up and holding it out to Kat.
"And here's for Matty."

Kat took the check and slipped it into her
jeans pocket. "Thank you so much."

Greta sat down in one of the two chairs
facing the desk and started rummaging through
her huge purse. "Imogene, since you're writing
checks at the moment, I've tallied up Harry's
total for last week."

Imogene winked at Kat as she resettled in
her chair. "All people want from me anymore is
money," she said, but her voice was laced with
mirth.

Greta held up a few pages printed on Cherry
Hills Veterinary letterhead. "I have the itemized
invoices here for your records."

Greta's hair had fallen into her face as she'd
turned her head down to sift through her purse,
and now she had to smooth the blond locks
back from her eyes. As Kat watched her bend

forward to place the invoices on Imogene's desk, she caught a glimpse of the woman's pro-file.

Kat's breath caught. From this angle, she had no trouble discerning the single, empty hole located in the fleshy part of Greta's ear, and the tear that stretched from the tiny piercing all the way to the bottom of her earlobe.

CHAPTER TEN

Kat drifted through her shift at Jessie's Diner in a fog, her mind on the events of the past few days. During a lull in business, she'd stepped outside and phoned Greta Opheim, asking her to stop by her apartment at six o'clock under the guise of discussing the Furry Friends Foster Families benefit dinner. Kat's fingers had been trembling when she'd disconnected the call.

Kat left Jessie's after the evening waitstaff took over. She made it home by 5:20 P.M., her heart beating faster and faster as the clock ticked toward six. When the doorbell finally rang two minutes after the hour, Kat's heart practically jumped out of her chest.

Kat approached the front door. She took a deep breath and rubbed her sweaty palms on her jeans before reaching for the doorknob.

"Hi, Kat," Greta greeted. "You wanted to talk about the 4F benefit?"

Kat forced herself to nod. "Come in."

Greta stepped over the threshold, and Kat closed the door behind her.

"Why don't you have a seat?" Kat said, sweeping her arm toward the living area.

"This is a nice place you've got here," Greta commented, taking a seat on one sofa.

Kat moved farther into the living room. "Thanks." Then, unable to maintain the charade, she turned toward Greta and blurted out, "I know you killed Mrs. Tinsdale."

Greta's face paled. "I—I have no idea what you're talking about."

"Sure you do," Kat replied. "I know you inflated the charges on the vet invoices you submitted to 4F. Mrs. Tinsdale found out about it, and she threatened to expose you, didn't she?"

Greta's face was as white as a ghost's now. Her tongue practically touched the floor as her mouth gaped open.

Kat walked over to the kitchen table and

picked up the Cherry Hills Veterinary invoices she had raced home to study during her lunch break at Jessie's. "These came from Mrs. Tinsdale's apartment," she said, waving the invoices in front of her. "She wrote some comments on the back."

"Comments?" Greta squeaked.

Kat flipped the top page over and read the note that Mrs. Tinsdale had penned. "She linked this invoice to a dog named Muffy, who's currently in foster care courtesy of 4F. She had a question as to why the bill includes charges for both the all-in-one parasite-prevention medicine and individual treatments against heartworm, roundworm, and the like." Kat looked at Greta. "That seems rather strange to me, too. Wouldn't a dog only need to be treated for the same parasite once?"

"In an ideal world, yes," Greta said, crossing her legs. "But you have to understand, these medications aren't foolproof. Combining the different options makes it that much more likely the recipient animal stays healthy."

Kat examined Greta. She had delivered the explanation in a strangely mechanical fashion, almost as if she had it memorized.

"If combining the treatments is so much

more effective, why didn't Dr. Harry suggest that Matty receive both medications when I took her into his office yesterday?" Kat challenged. "I would think he would have said something if what you're saying is true."

Greta ran one finger along the edge of the couch. "He probably assumed you were on a fixed budget, working at Jessie's Diner and all. The specialized medicine is a lot more costly."

Kat regarded her. "I don't believe you."

Greta lifted one shoulder. "It's true."

Kat set the invoices back on the kitchen table, freeing her hands to fish her cell phone out of her jeans pocket. "Then you won't mind if I call up your husband to verify."

"No!" Greta lunged, but Kat sidestepped her.

Kat stared at the blonde, surprised by her aggression. Greta's mouth had the same taut set to it that Kat had seen at Jessie's Diner on Tuesday. She had surmised then that she'd caught the Opheims in the middle of a marital disagreement, but perhaps Greta's perturbed expression had really resulted from her agitation over murdering a woman earlier that very morning.

"The jig is up, Greta," Kat said, slipping her

phone back in her pocket. "I saw your torn earlobe, and Matty found your lost earring in Mrs. Tinsdale's apartment. I'm guessing Mrs. Tinsdale ripped it off during your struggle in her bedroom."

Kat waited a moment to give Greta a chance to reply, but continued when the other woman didn't say anything.

"I also know the reason Matty went wild during her checkup was because she recognized you as Mrs. Tinsdale's killer. I had falsely assumed she was afraid of Dr. Harry, but *you* were the one holding down her cat carrier. She was terrified of you—naturally, as she witnessed you murdering her owner."

Greta remained silent, but when Kat saw her hands compress into tight fists she knew she'd struck a nerve.

"It won't do you any good to deny it," Kat said. "I have all the invoices Mrs. Tinsdale saved. And I have copies stored somewhere safe, so don't even think of destroying the ones here."

Greta's jaw clenched and unclenched several times before her face drooped. "Fine," she said, an edge to her voice. She threw her hands in the air. "Fine! You figured me out."

Kat reached behind her, bracing herself against the kitchen table. "Why did you do it? Why were you overcharging 4F?"

"Because they deserved it," Greta spat. "They were always taking advantage of Harry. Often he didn't even want to invoice them for his services, if you can believe that. I told him he had to, that that was our money. Eventually I convinced him to let me act as his liaison with 4F."

"But you belong to 4F yourself," Kat said. "You must see the value in your husband's donation of his time."

"I only joined so I would have more control within the organization," Greta said, her eyes flashing. "I thought I would have some influence over how they spent their money once I became part of the board, but that Hilda was such a control freak. She insisted she handle everything, and she never let anybody but Imogene near her books."

Knowing what she knew about Greta now, Kat had to silently admit that had been a wise decision on Mrs. Tinsdale's part—if you ignored the fact that that good decision had ended up getting her killed.

Greta's face reddened. "That little snot. I

told Hilda what each line item was for when she came to me with all her questions, nitpicking over every little charge on those invoices I'd fudged. But what did she do? She sent Harry a letter, asking for further clarification."

"How did Dr. Harry respond to that?" Kat asked.

"He never received her stupid letter. I intercepted it before he could read what she'd written." Greta paused. "Then I came over here that morning, planning to tell Hilda that if she didn't like the way Harry ran his practice she could take 4F's business elsewhere. That would have made both of us happy. Then Harry would have more time to see paying clients, and Hilda could go take advantage of the other local vets' charity."

"But she wouldn't let the issue go," Kat surmised. "She said if you were cheating people by fabricating charges, she had an obligation to report you."

"You should have heard her spiel." Greta snorted. "Like she was this high and mighty princess out to right everything wrong with the world."

Kat nodded. "It's enough to make anybody sane want to commit murder."

Greta's eyes narrowed as she shot Kat a nasty look. Then her shoulders sagged, the fight seeming to drain from her body. "Hilda surprised me when she fought back."

Kat tilted her head. "What exactly happened on Tuesday?"

"When I showed up that morning at Harry's practice, I saw Hilda's letter. Sherry had left it in his inbox, as she does with all the mail. I called Hilda right away and asked if I could come over to discuss it."

Kat remembered Andrew saying that Dr. Harry's number had been the last one listed in Mrs. Tinsdale's call history. Greta must have phoned using her husband's office line.

Greta's eyes glazed over. She seemed to be getting lost in her memory of that morning. "Hilda agreed to meet me, and when I arrived she led me into her bedroom where she had the invoices I'd given her last week."

Kat found herself holding her breath. She had to consciously inhale so she could focus on Greta's story without becoming dizzy.

"She started going on and on about her concerns that 4F was being overcharged. She used this haughty, pedantic tone, as if she were explaining something to a dimwitted child."

Greta scoffed. "I tried to reason with her, but she wasn't buying it. Then I told her if she didn't agree with the charges, 4F could just stop using Cherry Hills Veterinary altogether."

The room fell silent as Greta stopped talking. She looked down at her hands, wringing them together.

"But that wasn't enough for her," Greta finally said, her voice much softer now. "She said billing for services not rendered was immoral, illegal. She said she had an obligation to report fraud to the Better Business Bureau. I knew if I didn't keep her from talking, she would destroy Harry's reputation."

Kat swallowed. "So you attacked her."

Greta nodded slowly. "Hilda started grabbing at everything in reach—first the bedspread, then the lamp—as she tried to get away. She made it into the bathroom, but there was nowhere left for her to go from there."

A sickness developed in the pit of Kat's stomach. She tried not to visualize the scene she'd stumbled across two days ago, but warding off the memory was impossible.

Greta took a deep breath. "At some point she hit her head on the toilet. Hard. I knew it was over then. So I gathered up the invoices that Hilda had pulled out to show me, planning to shred them at home." Her gaze moved to the kitchen table. "I didn't realize she had more stashed somewhere, but I wasn't thinking clearly enough to give it much thought. I just wanted to get out of there."

Kat would be eternally grateful that Greta hadn't gone in search of Mrs. Tinsdale's archived invoices. The inflated charges and Mrs. Tinsdale's notes not only helped to prove that Cherry Hills Veterinary had defrauded 4F, but established a motive for Greta to kill her fellow volunteer. Without the annotated invoices, Greta might have gotten away with her crimes.

A loud thump on the other side of Kat's apartment interrupted their conversation. Andrew emerged from the hallway. Two other officers followed behind him as he strode into the living room.

"Greta Opheim, you're under arrest for the murder of Hilda Tinsdale," Andrew said.

Greta's eyes widened. "You were listening this whole time?" She turned toward Kat, her face darkening.

Kat shrugged. "When I told him about my suspicions, he was the one who suggested hiding in my bedroom while I worked on coaxing you into a confession."

Greta looked as if she wanted to spit. Her eyes darted toward the police officers, and she said, "I want a lawyer."

"That's your right," Andrew replied. He motioned his supporting officers forward. "Cuff her and read her her rights. I'll meet you both at the station."

One of the officers secured Greta's wrists behind her back while the other recited her Miranda rights. She went willingly as they led her out of the apartment.

When Kat and Andrew were alone, she turned to face him. "You caught everything on tape?" she asked.

He smiled, his dimples indenting his cheeks. "Every last word."

Kat felt relief wash over her. "Combined with the earring and the invoices, you should have everything you need to prove her guilt, even if she pleads innocent."

"Yep," Andrew agreed. "But in case I'm wrong, we always have a secret eyewitness that we can trot into the courtroom."

Kat grinned. "I thought you said cats couldn't be eyewitnesses."

"I might just have to make an exception for

Matilda."

As if on cue, Matty ambled down the hallway. She'd been holed up in the bedroom along
with the police officers. Kat hadn't wanted to
subject her to another stressful encounter with
Greta Opheim.

Kat's heart surged with love as the feline approached. She crouched closer to Matty, bury-
ing her fingers in the cat's soft fur. "It looks like
your mama's going to get justice after all, girl."

CHAPTER ELEVEN

With Greta Opheim in jail awaiting trial, Kat and Andrew were celebrating over dinner at Jessie's Diner. Kat had the night off, and Andrew was authorized to use up a few vacation days after closing his first murder case. Kat had already promised Matty that she would return with whatever leftovers she could scrounge up so the feline didn't have to miss out on this evening's celebration.

It was Kat and Andrew's first meal together since they had run into each other the morning of Mrs. Tinsdale's murder. As they both munched on their burgers, Kat realized how much she'd missed his easy company. She had yet to meet another human being who made her feel as content as Andrew did.

"This brings back memories, huh?" Andrew grinned at her as he reached for his strawberry milkshake.

Kat tried to ignore the fluttering in her stomach inspired by that incredible smile. "It sure does. Only this time we're fully capable of paying for our milkshakes, thanks to my employee discount."

Andrew laughed.

"Yoo-hoo!"

Kat paused mid-dunk from dipping a french fry into a dollop of ketchup. Barreling toward them from the restaurant's front entrance was Imogene Little.

Imogene flew over to their table and plopped into the booth seat next to Kat without waiting for an invitation. "Kat Harper, I'm tickled to run into you here!"

Kat smiled. Although she was somewhat disappointed that her and Andrew's dinner had been interrupted, she was growing quite fond of the Furry Friends Foster Families president.

"Now that Hilda and Greta are no longer with us, I have a proposition for you," Imogene continued, not sparing Andrew a cursory glance. Kat wasn't even sure if she'd noticed him.

"What's that?" Kat asked, swishing her french fry back and forth.

Imogene shifted sideways, imploring Kat with her eyes. "We need somebody to fill in as 4F treasurer. I thought you'd be perfect for the job."

"I don't have any bookkeeping experience," Kat said.

Imogene flapped her hand. "Oh, we don't care about credentials. We just need somebody who cares about animals as much as we do. The treasury part is a small portion of what you'll do."

Kat absorbed Imogene's offer, her heart beating a little faster at the thought of accepting. She had always wanted to become more involved with animals but had never found the right time or opportunity. Volunteering at 4F would fulfill that desire.

"I'd love to," Kat told Imogene.

Imogene's eyes brightened. "That's fantastic! When can you start?"

Kat lifted one shoulder. "Anytime."

Imogene rubbed her palms together. "Oh, marvelous! We still have quite a bit to do before the benefit dinner next month. You can jump into that project right away. Come to our next meeting this Saturday at noon, my house. I'll tell you everything you need to know then."

Kat grinned. "Great."

As Imogene bustled off, Kat popped the french fry into her mouth. She didn't know exactly how demanding the treasurer position at 4F would be, but she knew one thing for certain.

Whatever the future had in store for Katherine Harper, she was pretty sure it would be adventurous.

NOTE FROM THE AUTHOR

Thank you for visiting Cherry Hills, home of Kat and Matty! If you enjoyed their story, please consider leaving a book review on your favorite retailer and/or review site.

Keep reading for an excerpt from Book Two of the Cozy Cat Caper Mystery series, *Framed in Cherry Hills*, and descriptions of some of the other books in the series. Thank you!

FRAMED
in CHERRY
HILLS

What happens when big trouble comes to a small town?

Cherry Hills resident Kat Harper doesn't expect her first meeting with the Furry Friends Foster Families animal rescue to kick off with the mysterious absence of another member. But it soon becomes clear why Willow Wu is a no-show; she's been arrested for a crime that nobody can believe.

Kat's convinced someone framed Willow. But who would do such a thing? A crooked small-town cop with big dreams? A local teenager looking for revenge? Or the disgruntled caterer who lost out on a lucrative job?

With this case hitting so close to home, Kat's determined to find the guilty party. And if she can cajole her cat Matty into lending another helping paw, the amateur detective might just succeed.

* * *

Please check your favorite online retailer for availability.

Excerpt From

FRAMED
in CHERRY
HILLS

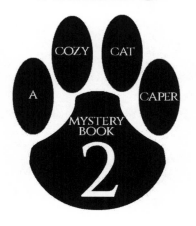

COZY CAT

A

CAPER

MYSTERY
BOOK

2

PAIGE SLEUTH

"Something is wrong," Imogene Little said, twining her fingers together. "Willow is never late."

Katherine Harper looked at the clock in Imogene's home office. "It's only twelve-fifteen. Maybe she got snagged in traffic."

Imogene shook her head, her auburn locks flying around her shoulders. "She would have called in that case. She would at least have picked up her phone when I called."

"Even if she were driving?"

Imogene nodded. "She has one of those fancy hands-free sets. Something must be wrong. It's the only possibility."

Kat wanted to say something to ease Imogene's concerns until they knew for sure what was going on, but, having never met Willow Wu, she found herself at a loss for words. This Saturday afternoon in July marked the first time she had planned to meet the third member of the Furry Friends Foster Families—or 4F, for short—nonprofit organization.

Kat looked uneasily out the window as the steady sound of rain beating against the house filled the room. A storm had been brewing ever since the night before, and this morning's rain hadn't let up yet. It was the type of weather conducive to traffic accidents, which made Willow's absence all the more worrisome. Still, Kat figured the possibility of a car wreck had already crossed Imogene's mind, and she could see no sense in bringing it up.

Imogene snatched up the cell phone on her desk and punched a few buttons before pressing it to her ear. After a moment she dropped the phone, shaking her head as she slumped into her seat. She didn't have to say anything for Kat to know that Willow had failed to answer Imogene's call once again.

A big, white cat sauntered into the room. He paused three feet past the doorway and studied Kat with his sky-blue eyes. He must have decided she was good for a few strokes because he ambled over and sat down within petting reach.

Kat leaned over and ran one hand down the animal's back. He felt so soft that she formed the impression she was stroking a cloud.

"That's Clover," Imogene said.

"Is he yours?" Kat didn't remember seeing Clover during a previous visit to Imogene's house, but she'd only been over once before. She had moved back to her hometown of Cherry Hills, Washington, just a few weeks ago, and, although Imogene had lived here when Kat had been growing up, she'd only struck up a friendship with the fifty-something woman recently.

"He's a foster," Imogene said. "He doesn't get along well with other cats. Since I was between animals, I was the only foster parent in a position to take him in."

"He's beautiful," Kat said as Clover pushed his nose into her palm.

Imogene beamed. "Isn't he, though? I'm tempted to adopt him myself, except that would mandate that I stop fostering other animals."

"Couldn't you keep him separated from any fosters you took in?"

Imogene laughed, looking at the white cat fondly. "I don't think Clover would go for that. He seems to believe he owns the entire house."

Imogene's cell phone rang, causing them both to straighten.

"That must be Willow." Imogene scrambled for the phone. "Hello?"

Having apparently had his fill of attention, Clover wandered over to an armchair on the other side of the room, jumped into the seat, and circled around once before settling down.

"Oh, I'm terribly sorry about that, Paul."

The worry in Imogene's voice sent a prickle of fear through Kat's body. She stilled as she listened to Imogene's half of the phone conversation.

"I don't know." Imogene fingered the edge of her desk with her free hand. "She was due here at noon, but she hasn't shown up yet. I didn't realize she'd already missed another appointment." She fell silent for a moment, then bobbed her head. "Yes, of course. I'll do that. Thank you, and I'll see you soon."

Kat leaned forward, trying to keep her dread at bay as Imogene pulled her phone away from her ear. "Who was that?"

"Paul McGinty." The cell phone slipped out of Imogene's hand, landing with a thunk on the desk. "Evidently Willow was supposed to stop by his house half an hour ago so he could talk to her about Tom."

"Who's Tom?"

"One of our foster cats. The McGintys are currently caring for him until he finds a permanent home."

"Ah."

Imogene chewed the edge of her lip. "Wherever Willow is, something dreadful must have happened. She never misses appointments without at least calling."

Kat glanced out the window, shivering as she watched the rain pelting the glass panes. Although it was still early afternoon, the darkening skies gave the impression that the hour was closer to nighttime.

Imogene jumped out of her chair, seeming to have gotten a fresh burst of energy. "Anyway, I've got to head over to Paul's. He sounded pretty upset that Willow didn't show when she said she would."

Kat stood up. "Should I come with you?"

Imogene's face brightened. "Yes, that would be wonderful. This way you'll get to experience firsthand some of what we do here at 4F."

"Sounds good." Kat grabbed her purse off the floor and followed Imogene out the door.

Paige Sleuth

* * *

Please check your favorite online retailer for availability.

POISONED
in CHERRY
HILLS

Animal rescue can be a deadly business.

Murder is the last thing on Kat Harper's mind
when she shows up for the Furry Friends Foster
Families benefit dinner. But that's exactly what
she gets when one of the guests drops dead.
Now the focus of the evening has shifted from
cat adoptions to catching a killer.

Between an old childhood rival, a sister in line
to inherit everything, and a couple with opportunity aplenty, there's no shortage of suspects.
Kat's going to need all of her sleuthing skills if
she hopes to identify "whodunit" this time . . .

especially when her cats Matty and Tom turn the case on its head and force her to question everything that happened that tragic night.

* * *

Please check your favorite online retailer for availability.

VANISHED
in CHERRY
HILLS

Is it possible to track down someone who doesn't want to be found?

Kat Harper spent most of her childhood in foster care, being raised by strangers while the woman who gave her life quietly slipped into the shadows. Now in her thirties, Kat longs to locate the mother she barely remembers.

Little does she know, so do the police.

It turns out, Kat's mother is suspected of a crime that's gone unsolved for thirty years. And if Kat is successful in her quest, her mother might reenter her life only to spend her remaining years behind bars.

Torn between her greatest wish and her biggest fear, Kat's not sure what to do. Living in darkness for another thirty years isn't an option, but will her need for answers end up forever alienating the one person she yearns to connect with most?

* * *

Please check your favorite online retailer for availability.

SHOT
in CHERRY
HILLS

Animal rescue with a side of murder.

What starts off as a foster dog wellness check turns into a nightmare when a gunshot leads Kat Harper to a man's dead body. Eric Halstead's killer is gone by the time Kat arrives on the scene, but the amateur sleuth isn't about to let them get away that easily.

By all accounts, this homicide appears to be a neighborhood dispute turned deadly. And now it's up to Kat to determine exactly which neighbor pulled the trigger. Was it the do-it-yourself handyman who didn't appreciate Eric's frequent noise complaints? Or could it have been the local newspaper thief who swears he knows something relevant to the murder but refuses to talk to the police? And Kat certainly can't discount the loudmouthed older gentleman who seems to have a not-always-popular opinion about everything.

Kat might not know "whodunit" yet, but she knows one thing for sure. There's a lot more than justice riding on this case. With Eric's death comes the need to rehome his beloved tuxedo cat. And if Kat's not careful, this animal rescue mission may end with the newly orphaned feline falling into the hands of a cold-blooded killer.

* * *

Please check your favorite online retailer for availability.

ABOUT THE AUTHOR

Paige Sleuth is a pseudonym for mystery author Marla Bradeen. She plots murder during the day and fights for mattress space with her two rescue cats at night. When not attending to her cats' demands, she writes. Find her at: http://www.marlabradeen.com

Manufactured by Amazon.ca
Bolton, ON

41296771R00088